This Book
Was Donated By

Katie
McLaughlin

# Prudy's Problem

## and How She Solved It

# Prudy's Problem

## and How She Solved It

written and illustrated by

## Carey Armstrong-Ellis

HARRY N. ABRAMS, INC., PUBLISHERS

Prudy seemed like a normal little girl.
She had a sister. She had a dog.
She had two white mice.
She had a mom and a dad and her own room at home.

Yes, Prudy seemed normal.

But Prudy collected things.

Now most kids collect something.
Prudy's friend Egbert
collected butterflies.

So did Prudy.

Belinda had a stamp collection.

So did Prudy.

Harold collected tin foil and made it into a big ball.

So did Prudy.

SCIENCE
C+

All her friends had collections.
And so did Prudy—
but Prudy collected *everything*.

She saved rocks, feathers, leaves, twigs, dead bugs, and old flowers. She kept a box full of interesting fungi in the bottom drawer of her dresser. She saved every picture she had ever drawn, and every valentine she had ever gotten. She saved pretty paper napkins from parties and kept them in her desk drawer. She had six hundred and fourteen stuffed animals in different unnatural colors.

She had collections of ribbons, shoelaces, souvenir postcards, flowered
fabric scraps, pencils with fancy ends, pink scarves with orange polka
dots, old calendars, salt and pepper shakers with faces, dried-out erasers,
plastic lizards, pointy sunglasses, china animals, heart-shaped candy
boxes with the paper candy cups still inside, tufts of hair from
different breeds of dogs....

She just could not throw anything away.

It drove her dad to distraction. He was a
very tidy person who did not like clutter.
He started saying unpleasant things as he
tried to mow the lawn.

"Prudy, you have a problem," he said.

"What do you mean?" she asked, baffled.

"You just have too much stuff. Why don't we
haul it all to the dump?" he suggested hopefully.

"I don't have too much stuff, Dad," Prudy said.

It even got to be too much for her mom, who did not mind clutter but could no longer navigate the living room.

"Maybe you could take all this to the thrift shop," she said. "Surely someone could use this old mushroom...."

"I *like* that mushroom," Prudy said.

"Prudy, you have to face your problem," said her mother.

"I do not have a problem," said Prudy.

Prudy's little sister started putting together collections of her own.

"Uh-oh," said Egbert, eyeing Evie's little piles of pine twigs and used toothbrushes. "Prudy, how about if you packed everything all up and stuffed it into a rocket and sent it to Neptune?"

"Yeah, that would solve your problem!" agreed Harold and Belinda.

"*There is no problem!*" shouted Prudy.

But Prudy herself found that she could
barely get to her desk to feed her mice.

She could not even get out of her room without
setting off an avalanche of one thing or another.

And then one day while Prudy was walking home from school,
something shiny caught her eye. It was a silver gum wrapper.
"I must take this home for my shiny things collection!" she thought.

She ran home and tried to squeeze it into her room.

Something started to happen. The walls started to bulge.
The door started to strain at the hinges.
The pressure was building higher...and higher...

The room exploded with an enormous BANG!

Bits and pieces of stuff flew everywhere.

"Holy smokes," said Prudy.
"I guess maybe I do have a little problem."

For six weeks, everyone pitched in to
gather Prudy's scattered collections.
"Now what, Prudy?" said her family.
"Now what, Prudy?" said her friends.
"I'm working on it!" said Prudy.

Prudy looked around for inspiration.
She visited an art collection.

She visited a fish collection.

She visited a rock collection.

She went to the library to find ideas.
At last, after many hours of scrutinizing
stacks of books, she came up with a brilliant plan!

With saws whirring and
hammers pounding,
everyone set to work.

ENTRANCE

tour guide

The Prudy Museum of Indescribable
Wonderment was an amazing
sight to behold.
Everyone wanted to go visit!

Cheese Rinds
of the World

Strange
Vegetables

Within a year, it was the biggest
tourist attraction in Prudy's town.

"Look at that, Egbert," said
Belinda. "Did you ever realize how
many kinds of gym socks there are?"

"I had no idea cheese rinds could
be so fascinating!" said Prudy's
mother.

"Can I go to the gift shop?"
said Evie.

At last Prudy's collections were neat and orderly and appreciated by everyone. Now she could sit back and enjoy the museum and all her happy visitors....

But she could never *really* stop collecting!

museum
storage
employees
only

To Erin and Emmy, my master collectors.
They inspired this book.

*Author's Note*

As a child, I had collections of many things: mice (not real), insects (real), toadstools (very real, unfortunately).
I even had an impressive collection of cast-off cicada shells. As an adult, I was fascinated to watch my children,
with no encouragement from me or my long-suffering husband, start making collections of their own.
Fascination turned to alarm, though, as their collective tendencies far surpassed mine. We have not, as yet, found a solution.

Generally I work with fabric in my art. But making a fabric sculpture is very time-consuming and complicated, and looks it.
For *Prudy's Problem* I wanted the art to look funny, fresh, and spontaneous. So, for the first time,
I turned to paper and paint. The pictures are done in gouache and colored pencil. First I sketched out my ideas in pencil,
working out all the details of Prudy's many collections. Then, to make the final art, I made new drawings in pencil and
painted in with gouache for the main colors. Finally, I went over everything in colored pencil to bring out the details.
It was fun to try something that gave more immediate results than my usual methods. I hope that young collectors
everywhere will enjoy *Prudy's Problem*—and that Prudy's resourcefulness will give them some ideas on getting
their own collections under control. Even if their rooms are just the way they like them.

—Carey Armstrong-Ellis

Designer: Becky Terhune

Library of Congress Cataloging-in-Publication Data

Armstrong-Ellis, Carey.
Prudy's problem and how she solved it / by Carey Armstrong-Ellis.
p. cm.
Summary: Prudy collects so many things that everyone says she has a problem,
but when a crisis convinces her that they are right, she comes up with the perfect solution.
ISBN 0-8109-0569-8
[1. Collectors and collecting--Fiction. 2. Museums--Fiction.]
I. Title.
PZ7.A73396 Pr 2002
[E]--dc21
2001006903

Printed and bound in Hong Kong

10 9 8 7 6 5 4 3 2 1

Harry N. Abrams, Inc.
100 Fifth Avenue
New York, N.Y. 10011
www.abramsbooks.com

Abrams is a subsidiary of

LA MARTINIÈRE
GROUPE